Songs from the Garden of Eden

JEWISH LULLABIES
AND NURSERY RHYMES

SONGS COLLECTED BY NATHALIE SOUSSANA
MUSICAL ARRANGEMENTS BY PAUL MINDY
AND JEAN-CHRISTOPHE HOARAU
ILLUSTRATIONS BY BEATRICE ALEMAGNA

Erev shel shoshanim

1

An evening of roses
Come let us go into the garden
The scent of frankincense and myrrh
Enveloping your feet

Night falls slowly
A rose-scented breeze gently blows
I will whisper a song to you
A song of love

A dove coos at dawn
Your curls shimmer with dew
Your lips are like a rose in the morning
I will pick it for myself

Night falls slowly…

Erev shel shoshanim
Netse na el hab oustan
Mor besamim oulevona
Leraglekh miftan

Layla yored le'at
Verouah shoshan noshva
Hava elhash lakh shir balat
Zemer shel ah'ava

Shahar homa yona
Roshekh mal e tlalim
Pikh el haboker shoshana
Ektefenou li

Layla yored le'at…

עֶרֶב שֶׁל שׁוֹשַׁנִּים נֵצֵא נָא אֶל הַבֻּסְתָּן
מוֹר בְּשָׂמִים וּלְבוֹנָה לְרַגְלֵךְ מִפְתָּן

לַיְלָה יוֹרֵד לְאַט וְרוּחַ שׁוֹשָׁן נוֹשְׁבָה
הָבָה אֶלְחַשׁ לָךְ שִׁיר בַּלְאַט זֶמֶר שֶׁל אַהֲבָה

שַׁחַר הוֹמָה יוֹנָה, רֹאשֵׁךְ מָלֵא טְלָלִים
פִּיךְ אֶל הַבֹּקֶר שׁוֹשַׁנָה אֶקְטְפֶנּוּ לִי

לַיְלָה יוֹרֵד לְאַט

Hebrew
Lyrics Moshe Dor Music Yosef Hadar
Singers Laura Drouillard and Awena Burgess

Alevanta Sultanatchi

2

Get up Sultanatchi, aman	Alevanta Sultanatchi, aman
Get up, you must eat	Alevanta komeràs
Leave me alone father, aman	Ke me deche sinyor padre, aman
Leave me alone with my pain	Ke me deche kon mi mal
Sultanatchi ran off to the baths, aman	Sultanatchi se fue al banyo, aman
With the Rabbi's daughter	Kon la ija del haham
When Rubenatchi saw her, aman	Rubenatchi ke la vidò, aman
He went after her to slap her	La korryò para aharvar

Judeo-Spanish
Traditional, musical arrangement Christophe Hoarau
and Paul Mindy Singer Awena Burgess

A la una

3

At one I was born	A la una yo nasì
At two I grew up	A las dos m'engrandesì
At three I took a lover	A las tres tomì amante
At four I married	A las kuatro me kazì
Tell me little girl	- Dime ninya d'ànde vyenes?
Where do you come from?	
	Ke te kyero konoser
Because I want to get to know you	I si no tyenes amante
If you have no lover	Yo te arè defender
I will defend you	Yèndome para la gerra
As I set off to war	Dos bezos al ayre di
I throw kisses into the air	El uno es para mi madre
One is for my mother	I el otro para ti
And the other is for you	

Judeo-Spanish
Traditional, musical arrangement Christophe Hoarau and Paul Mindy
Singers Laura Drouillard, Awena Burgess, Gabrielle Maalouli and Avran Thepault

4 Dona, dona

שרײַט דאָס קעלבל, זאָגט דער פּויער,
ווער זשע הייסט דיך זײַן אַ קאַלב ?
וואָלסט געקערט צו זײַן אַ פֿויגל,
וואָלסט געקערט צו זײַן אַ שוואַלב.

בידנע קעלבלעך טוט מען בינדן,
און מען שלעפּט זיי און מען שעכט.
ווער ס'האָט פֿליגל פֿליט אַרויף צו,
איז בײַ קיינעם נישט קיין קנעכט !

אויפֿן פֿורל ליגט אַ קעלבל,
ליגט געבונדן מיט אַ שטריק.
הויך אין הימל פֿליט אַ פֿויגל,
פֿליט און דרייט זיך הין און צריק.

לאַכט דער ווינט אין קאָרן,
לאַכט און לאַכט און לאַכט,
לאַכט ער אָפּ אַ טאָג אַ גאַנצן,
און אַ האַלבע נאַכט.
דאָנאַ, דאָנאַ, דאָנאַ,
דאָנאַ, דאָנאַ, דאָן,
דאָנאַ, דאָנאַ, דאָנאַ,
דאָנאַ, דאָנאַ, דאָנאַ.

On a wagon bound for market
There's a calf with a mournful eye
High above him, there's a swallow
Winging swiftly through the sky

How the winds are laughing
They laugh with all their might
Laugh and laugh the whole day through
And half the summer's night
Dona, dona, dona, dona…

"Stop complaining," said the farmer,
"Who told you to be a calf?
Why don't you have wings to fly away
Like the sparrow so proud and free?
Calves are easily bound and slaughtered
Not knowing the reason why
But whoever treasures freedom
Like the swallow must learn to fly"

Oyfn furl ligt a kelbl
Ligt gebundn mit a shtrik
Hoykh in himl flit a foygl
Flit un dreyt zikh hin un tsrik

Lakht der vint in korn
Lakht un lakht un lakht
Lakht er op a tog a gantsn
Un a halbe nacht
Dona, dona, dona, dona…

Schrayt dos kelbl, zogt der poyer
Ver zhe heyst dikh zayn a kalb?
Volst gekert tsu zayn a foygl
Volst gekert tsu zayn a schvalb?
Bidne kelblekh tut men bindn
Un men shlept zey un men shekht
Ver s'hot fligl flit aroyf tsu
Iz bay keynem nisht keyn knecht

Yiddish
Lyrics Aaron Zeitlin Music Sholom Secunda
Singers Muriel Hirschman and Juliet Hoarau

Ikh bin a kleyner dreydl

5

I am a little dreydl	Ikh bin a kleyner dreydl
I am made of lead	Gemakht bin ikh fun blay
Come let us all play	Kumt, lomir ale shpiln
At dreydl, one, two, three	In dreydl, eyns, tsvey, dray
Oh, dreydl, dreydl, dreydl	Oy, dreydl, dreydl, dreydl
Oh spin dreydl spin	Oy, drey zik-h, dreydl, drey
So let all of us play	To lomir ale shpiln
At dreydl, one and two	In dreydl, eyns un tsvey
And I love to dance	Un ikh hob lib tsu tantsn
To twirl in a circle	Zikh dreyen in a rod
Come let us all dance	Kumt, lomir ale tantsn
A dreydl-round-dance	A dreydl-karahod

Yiddish
Lyrics Ben Arn Music Michl Gelbart
Singers Muriel Hirschman and Myriam Molinet

איך בין אַ קליינער דריידל
געמאַכט בין איך פֿון בלײַ.
קומט, לאָמיר אַלע שפילן
אין דריידל, איינס, צוויי, דרײַ.

אוי, דריידל, דריידל, דריידל,
אוי, דריי זיך, דריידל, דריי,
טאָ לאָמיר אַלע שפילן
אין דריידל, איינס און צוויי.

און איך האָב ליב צו טאַנצן,
זיך דרייען אין אַ ראָד.
קומט, לאָמיר אַלע טאַנצן
אַ דריידל-קאַראַהאָד.

Der zeyher

6

English	Transliteration	Yiddish
I am a clock hanging on the wall	Kh'bin a zeyger oyf der vant	כ׳בין אַ זייגער אויף דער וואַנט
And I chime regularly	Un ikh kling alts nokhanand	און איך קלינג אַלץ נאָכאַנאַנד,
Tick tock, tick tock	tik tak, tik tak	טיק טאַק טיק טאַק.
Although I talk all day long	Khotsh ikh red a gantsn tog	כאָטש איך רעד אַ גאַנצן טאָג
I only say two words	Bloyz tsvey verter kh'zog un zog	בלויז צוויי ווערטער כ׳זאָג און זאָג,
Tick tock, tick tock	tik tak, tik tak	טיק טאַק טיק טאַק.
Sometimes the children stay up late	Treft az kinder zitsn shpet	טרעפֿט אַז קינדער זיצן שפּעט,
I chime the bedtime hour	Kling ikh tsayt shoyn geyn in bet	קלינג איך צײַט שוין גיין אין בעט,
Tick tock, tick tock	tik tak, tik tak	טיק טאַק טיק טאַק
And I wake them when	Un ikh vek zey oyf in tsayt	און איך וועק זיי אויף אין צײַט,
The time has come	Loz nit lign oyf a zayt	לאָז ניט ליגן אויף אַ זײַט,
I never forget	tik tak, tik tak	טיק טאַק טיק טאַק,
Tick tock, tick tock		
I have been hanging here	Azoy heng ikh yorn lang	אַזוי הענג איך יאָרן לאַנג
Many long years	Mitn zelbikn gezang	מיטן זעלביקן געזאַנג,
Always chiming the same chorus	tik tak, tik tak	טיק טאַק טיק טאַק.
Tick tock, tick tock		

Yiddish
Traditional, musical arrangement
Christophe Hoarau and Paul Mindy
Singer Isabelle Marx

The new mother said:
"I am dying, I am dying"
Her husband replied:
"Be patient, my wife
You will bring a son
Into the world
And we will rejoice
For this joy is a good omen"

May the new mother live
And her life be a good one!

The young father arrives
With hands laden
In one he carries
Apples and pears
In the other
A handful of candles
To light the entire
Household

Turn, young mother
Towards the window
You will hear the young father
Reciting the She'he'chiyanu

Dichù la parida :
- Mi mueru, mi mueru
Arrespondyù il maridu :
- Pasensya mi mujer
Mi parirech un iju
I mus alegraremus
Sea buen siman esta
Alegriya

Ke mus biva la parida
I ke tenga buena vida!

Ya vyene il paridu
Kun manus yenas
In una manu yeva
Mansanas i peras
In la otra manu yeva
Un masu di kandelas
Para ke arrelumbri toda
la parintera

Aboltavoch parida
Para il verandadu
Sentirech il paridu
Dizyendu Cheeiyanu

Judeo-Spanish
Traditional, musical arrangement Christophe Hoarau
and Paul Mindy **Singer** Norig Recher

Tchiko Ianiko

8

Little Ianiko, the little bird
Made us borrekas*
With butter and cheese

Little Ianiko, the little bird
With a pastry roller and flour
Made a fine dough

Tchiko Ianiko, komu il pachariko
Ya mus fazi las borrekas*
Kun il kezu i la manteka

Tchiko Ianiko, komu il pachariko
Kun la fletcha i la farina
Sta faziendu masa fina

Judeo-Spanish
Lyrics and music Flory Jagoda Singer Nathalie Soussana

*Borrekas: culinary specialty, a type of cheese puff

La serena

9

If the sea was milk
I would become a merchant
Searching and asking
Where love begins

In the sea is a tower
In the tower is a window
In the window is a girl
Who calls to sailors

Give me your hand, my dove
So that I may climb to your nest
Unlucky is the person who sleeps alone
I am coming to sleep with you

If the sea was milk
I would be a fisherman
I would fish for my sorrows
With words of love

Judeo-Spanish
Traditional, musical arrangement Christophe Hoarau
and Paul Mindy Singer Awena Burgess

Si la mar era de letche
Yo me ariya vendedor
Kaminando i preguntando
Dònde s'ampesa l'amor

En la mar ay una torre
En la torre ay una ventana
En la ventana una ninya
Ke a los marineros yama

Dame la mano palomba
A suvir a tu lado
Malditcha ke durmes sola
Vengo a durmir kon ti

Si la mar era de letche
Yo me ariya peskador
Peskando los mis dolores
Kon palavrikas d'amor

Shuster

10

Shoemaker, shoemaker, quick, quick, quick
Take my old shoes
I will count one, two, three
And you make them new

Shuster, shuster, gikh, gikh, gikh
Na dir mayne alte shikh
Ven ikh tseyl op eyns, tsvey, dray
Zolstu mir zey makhn nay

שוסטער, שוסטער, גיך, גיך, גיך,
נאַ דיר מײַנע אַלטע שיך.
ווען איך צייל אָפּ איינס, צוויי, דרײַ,
זאָלסטו מיר זיי מאַכן נײַ.

Yiddish
Traditional, musical arrangement
Christophe Hoarau and Paul Mindy
Singer Isabelle Marx

A fidler

11

My father from the fair
Brought me a new fiddle

Do re mi fa sol la ti
I play tiddel di di di

I lower my head
Open my eyes wide

Move my right foot a little forward
And tap the beat with my little foot

My mother marvels in amazement:
How well you can play!

S'hot der tate fun yaridl
Mir gebrakht a naye fidl

Do re mi fa sol la si
Shpil ikh : tidl di di di

Kh'halt dos kepl ongeboygn
Un farglots di beyde oygn

Rekhtn trit foroys a bisl
Klapt dem takt tsu mitn fisl

Kvelt un vundert zikh di mame:
- Kenst dokh azoy gut di game!

Yiddish
Lyrics Shmuel Tsesler Music Hersh Wolowitz
Singer Isabelle Marx

ס'האָט דער טאַטע פֿון יאַרידל
מיר געבראַכט אַ נײַע פֿידל,

דאָ רע מי פֿאַ סאָל לאַ סי,
שפֿיל איך : טיד'ל'אי די די.

כ'האַלט דאָס קעפֿל אָנגעבויגן
און פֿאַרגלאָץ די ביידע אויגן.

רעכטן טריט פֿאָרויס אַ ביסל,
קלאַפֿט דעם טאַקט צו מיטן פֿיסל.

קוועלט און ווונדערט זיך די מאַמע :
„קענסט דאָך אַזוי גוט די גאַמע.‟

Durme, durme

12

Sleep, sleep my darling little boy
Sleep, sleep free of worry and pain
Close your pretty little eyes
Sleep softly

You will leave your swaddling clothes
You will go to school
And there, my darling little boy
You will learn the alphabet

You will leave school
You will go to the market
And there, my darling little boy
You will learn to sell

You will leave the market
You will go to university
And there, my darling little boy
You will become a doctor

Durme, durme ermozo ijiko
Durme, durme sin ansia i dolor
Serra tus lindos ojikos
Durme kon savor

De las fachas saliràs
A la echkola te iràs
I ayì mi kerido ijiko
Alef-Bet ambezaràs

De la echkola saliràs
A la plasa te iràs
I ayì mi kerido ijiko
Merkansiya ambezaràs

De la plasa saliràs
Al estudyo te iràs
I ayì mi kerido ijiko
Doktoriko saliràs

Judeo-Spanish
Traditional, musical arrangement Christophe Hoarau
and Paul Mindy Singer Norig Recher

13 Otcho kandelikas

Beautiful Chanukkah is here
Eight candles for me

One candle, two candles
Three candles, four candles
Five candles, six candles
Seven candles, eight candles for me

Hanuka linda sta aki, otcho
kandelas para mi

O, una kandelika, dos kandelikas
Tres kandelikas, kuatro kandelikas
Sinku kandelikas, sech kandelikas
Syete kandelikas, otcho kandelas para mi

Judeo-Spanish
Lyrics and music Flory Jagoda Singers Gabrielle Maalouli,
Laura Drouillard, Avran Thepault and Nathalie Soussana

14 Khanuke

אָ חנוכה, אָ חנוכה, אַ יום־טוב אַ שיינער
אַ לוסטיקער, אַ פֿריילעכער, ניטאָ נאָך אַזוינער,
אַלע נאַכט אין דריידלעך שפּילן מיר,
זודיק־הייסע לאַטקעס עסט אָן אַ שיר.

געשווינדער, צינדט קינדער,
די דיניקע ליכטעלעך אָן,
זאָגט על־הנסים,
לויבט גאָט פֿאַר די נסים
און קומט גיכער טאַנצן אין קאָן.

Oh Chanukkah, oh Chanukkah, what a beautiful celebration
Joyful and gay, there is nothing to match it
Every night we play with dreydls
And eat steaming hot latkes

Quickly, children, light
The small slender candles
Say "Praise God!"
For his "miracles"
And let the dancing begin

O khanuke, o khanuke, a yontef a sheyner
A lustiker, a freylekher, nito nokh azoyner
Ale nakht in dreydlekh shpiln mir
Zudik-heyse latkes est on a shir

Geshvinder, tsint kinder
Di dininke likhtelekh on
Zogt al-hanisim
Loybt got far di nisim
Un kumt gikher tantsn in kon

Yiddish
Traditional, musical arrangement Christophe Hoarau
and Paul Mindy Singer Esther Bluwol

15 Bibhilou

בְּבְהִילוּ יָצָאנוּ מִמְּצָרַיִם
הָא לַחְמָא עַנְיָא
בְּנֵי חוֹרִין.

God has led us out of Egypt
See the bread of suffering
We are free

Bibhilou yahtsanou mimitsraim
Ha lahma anya
Béné horin

Hebrew
Traditional, musical arrangement Christophe Hoarau
and Paul Mindy Singers Anita Soussana, Nathalie Soussana,
Patrick Assoune, Paul Mindy, Avran Thepault
and Milena Thepault

15 Etmol

אֶתְמוֹל הָיִינוּ עֲבָדִים
הַיּוֹם בְּנֵי חוֹרִין
הַיּוֹם כַּאן
לְשָׁנָה הַבָּאָה בִּרוּשָׁלַיִם.

Yesterday we were slaves
Today we are free
Today we are here
Tomorrow we will be in Jerusalem

Etmol hayinou avadim
Hayom béné horin
Hayom kan
Léchana haba'a Birouchalaïm

Hebrew
Traditional, musical arrangement Christophe Hoarau
and Paul Mindy Singers Anita Soussana, Nathalie Sous
Patrick Assoune, Paul Mindy, Avran Thepault
and Milena Thepault

5 Lekha dodi

Come, my beloved, and meet the bride
And welcome Sabbath
"Observe" and "recall" is but one word
We were made to hear by the unifying God
God is one and God's name is one
In fame and splendour and song
Come in peace, crown of your husband
Come my beloved in happiness and in jubilation
Among my faithful people
Come O Bride! Come O Bride!

Lekha dodi likrat kala
Péné Shabbat néka bela
"Chamor vézakhor" bédibour éhad
Hichmianou el haméyouhad :
"Ado-naï éhad ouchmo éhad"
Léchém oultiférèt vélitéhila
Boï véchalom atérét baalah
Gam bérina bésimha ouvétsahola
Tokh' émouné am ségoula
Boï khala boï khala

Hebrew
Poem Rabbi Salomon Alkabets Ha Levi
Musical arrangement Christophe Hoarau **and** Paul Mindy
Singers Anita Soussana, Nathalie Soussana, Patrick Assoune,
Paul Mindy, Avran Thepault **and** Milena Thepault

Tchichi Bunitchi

16

Tchitchi* Bunitchi
Little lord of the ring**
This one asks for bread
And this one asks for cheese
And if this one is not a good Jew
We will call Mr. Rabbi

Tchitchi Bunitchi
Little lord of the ring
This one says "Give me a small bag
The little hen has laid a little egg
Here, here, here, over here
In the mouth of my beloved daughter

Tchitchi* Bunitchi
I redi lanitchi**
Esti dimanda pan
Esti dimanda kezu
I esti si no es buen djidiyò
Vamus a yamar al sinyor Rubì

Tchitchi Bunitchi
I redi lanitchi
Esti dizi dami un paketiko
La gayinika etchò un guviziko
Aki, aki, aki, para aki
A la bokita di mi ijika

Judeo-Spanish
Traditional, musical arrangement Christophe Hoarau and Paul Mindy
Singers Gabrielle Maalouli, Laura Drouillard, Avran Thepault and Norig Recher

* Nickname given to the little finger
** Corruption of "rey del anitchi" (lord of the ring)

Nani, nani

17

Sleep, sleep, sleepy child, mother's child
Little one you'll grow up soon enough
Oh, sleep my soul, sleep apple of my eye
Because your father is returning all happy

Ah, wife, open the door, open up!
I'm back and tired from working the fields
I will not open the door: you are not tired at all
You are back from visiting your new love

Nani, nani, nani kere el ijo, el ijo de la madre
De tchiko se aga grande
Ay, durmite mi alma, durmite mi vista
Ke tu padre vyene kon muntcha alegriya

Ay, avrimes, mi dama, avrimes la puerta!
Ke vengo kansado de arar las uertas
Avrir no vos avro, no venich kansado
Sino ke venich de onde muevo amor

Judeo-Spanish
Traditional, musical arrangement Christophe Hoarau
and Paul Mindy Singer Awena Burgess

18 Yome, Yome

יאָמע, יאָמע, שפיל מיר אַ לידעלע,
וואָס דאָס מיידעלע וויל.
דאָס מיידעלע וויל אַ פּאָר שיכעלעך האָבן,
מוז מען גיין דעם שוסטער זאָגן.

Yome, Yome, sing me a song
Of what the little girl wants
The girl wants a pair of shoes
So we have to go to the shoemaker!

- Yome, Yome, shpil mir a lidele
Vos dos meydele vil
- Dos meydele vil a por shikhelekh hobn
Muz men geyn dem shuster zogn!

ניין, מאַמעשי, ניין,
דו קענסט מיך ניט פֿאַרשטיין,
דו ווייסט ניט וואָס איך מיין.

No, mama, no!
You don't understand me
You don't know what I want!

- Neyn, mameshi, -neyn!
Du kenst mikh nit farshteyn
Du veyst nit, vos ikh meyn!

דאָס מיידעלע וויל אַ היטעלע האָבן,
מוז מען גיין דער פּוצערקע זאָגן.

...The girl wants a hat
So we have to go to the milliner!

… Dos meydele vil a hitele hobn
Muz men geyn dem putserke zogn!

דאָס מיידעלע וויל אַ חתדל האָבן,
מוז מען גיין דעם שדכן זאָגן.

… The girl wants a groom
So we have to go to the matchmaker!

… Dos meydele vil a khosndl hobn
Muz men geyn dem shadkhn zogn!

יאָ, מאַמעשי, יאָ,
דו קענסט מיך שוין פֿאַרשטיין,
דו ווייסט שוין וואָס איך מיין.

Yes, mama, yes!
At last you understand me
At last you know what I want!

- Yo, mameshi, yo!
Du kenst mikh shoyn farshteyn
Du veyst shoyn vos ikh meyn!

Yiddish
Traditional, musical arrangement Christophe Hoarau
and Paul Mindy Singers Milena Thepault
and Nathalie Soussana

Yankele

19

Sleep, sleep Yankele, my handsome son
Close your little black eyes
My little one, now that you have all your teeth
Must you make your mother sing you to sleep?

A little boy who has all his teeth
And who will soon go to school
And learn Torah and Talmud
Must he cry when his mama rocks him to sleep?

A little boy who will learn to read
And make his father very proud
A little boy who will be so smart
Must he keep his mother awake all night?

A little boy who will be so smart
And be a brilliant shopkeeper
A little boy old enough to be engaged
Must he stay in his bed, all wet?

Sleep, then, my handsome groom
Sleep while you are still in your cradle by my side
Your mother will shed many tears
Before she makes a man of you

Shlof zhe mir shoyn Yankele, mayn sheyner
Di eygelekh di shvartsinke makh tsu
A yingele vos hot shoyn ale tseyndelekh
Muz nokh di mame zingen ay-lyu-lyu

A yingele vos hot shoyn ale tseyndelekh
Un vet mit mazl bald in kheyder geyn
Un lernen vet er khumesh mit gemore
Zol veynen ven di mame vigt im eyn?

A yingele vos lernen vet gemore
Ot shteyt der tate kvelt un hert zikh tsu
A yingele vos vakst a talmid-khokhem
Lozt gantse nekht der mamen nisht tsu ru?

A yingele vos vakst a talmid-khokhem
Un a geniter soykher oykh tsu glaykh
A yingele a kluger khosn-bokher
Zol lign azoy nas vi in a taykh

Nu shlof zhe mir, mayn kluger khosn-bokhe
Dervayl ligstu in vigele bay mir
S'vet kostn nokh fil mi un mames trern
Biz vanen s'vet a mentsh aroys fun dir

Yiddish
Lyrics and music Mordecai Gebirtig
Singers Esther Bluwol and Raphaële Lannadere

שלאָף זשע מיר שוין יאַנקעלע, מײַן שיינער,
די אייגעלעך די שוואַרצינקע מאַך צו.
אַ ייִנגעלע וואָס האָט שוין אַלע ציינדעלעך,
מוז נאָך די מאַמע זינגען אַיי-ליו-ליו.

אַ ייִנגעלע וואָס האָט שוין אַלע ציינדעלעך,
און וועט מיט מזל באַלד אין חדר גיין,
און לערנען וועט ער חומש מיט גמרא,
זאָל וויינען ווען די מאַמע וויגט אים אײַן ?

אַ ייִנגעלע וואָס לערנען וועט גמרא,
אָט שטייט דער טאַטע קוועלט און הערט זיך צו,
אַ ייִנגעלע וואָס וואַקסט אַ תּלמיד-חכם,
לאָזט גאַנצע נעכט דער מאַמען נישט צו רו ?

אַ ייִנגעלע וואָס וואַקסט אַ תּלמיד-חכם,
און אַ געניטער סוחר אויך צר גלײַך,
אַ ייִנגעלע אַ קלוגער חתן-בחור
זאָל ליגן אַזוי נאַס ווי אין אַ טײַך ?

נו שלאָף זשע מיר, מײַן קלוגער חתן-בחור,
דערווײַל ליגסטו אין וויגעלע בײַ מיר.
ס׳וועט קאָסטן נאָך פֿיל מי און מאַמעס טרערן
ביז וואַנען ס׳וועט אַ מענטש אַרויס פֿון דיר.

Sara la preta

20

The Black One	A Sara la preta
Lost her breast	Le kayò la teta
She searched and searched	Buchka, buchka
But could not find it	I no la topò
Her neighbour told her	Le dichò la vezina
To sweep the kitchen	Ke barra la kuzina
"Because you ate bread and kachkaval*"	Ke komites pan i kachkaval*
La la la la…	Lai la la la la …

Judeo-Spanish
Traditional, musical arrangement
Christophe Hoarau and Paul Mindy Singers Norig Recher, Avran
Thepault, Gabrielle Maalouli and Laura Drouillard

*Type of pressed cheese made of sheep's or cow's milk

Hachafan hakatan

21

The little rabbit
Forgot to close the door
The poor little thing caught a chill
And caught a cold
La la la achoo

Hachafan hakatan
Chakhah'lisgor hadelet
Hitstanen hamisken
Vekibel nazelet
La la la aptchi

הַשָּׁפָן הַקָטָן
שָׁכַח לִסְגֹּר הַדֶּלֶת
הִצְטַנֵן הַמִסְכֵּן
וְקִבֵּל נַזֶלֶת.
לָה לָה לָה אַפְצָ׳י.

Hebrew
Lyrics Benjamin Caspi
Musical arrangement Christophe Hoarau and Paul Mindy
Singers Avran Thepault and Milena Thepault

Lyalkele

22

Little doll, little doll, go to sleep
Your mother is rocking you now

She is singing you to sleep with a little song
Be well, do it for me
Baby birds sleep in their little nest
Close your tiny eyes, little doll, little doll

ליאַלקעלע, ליאַלקעלע, אַיַ־ליו־ליו,
דײַן מאַמע וויגט דיך איצטער צו.

Lyalkele, lyalkele, ay-lyu-lyu
Dayn mame vigt dikh itster tsu

מיט אַ לידעלע שלעפֿט זי דיך אײַן,
זאָלסטו מיר אַ געזונטע זײַן.

Mit a lidele shleft zi dikh ayn
Zolstu mir a gezunte zayn
In nestl shlofn di feygelekh
Farmakh zhe dayne eygelekh

אין נעסטל שלאָפֿן די פֿייגעלעך,
פֿאַרמאַך זשע דײַנע אייגעלעך.

Yiddish
Lyrics A. Moshkowitch Music Leon Dreytzel
Singers Muriel Hirschman and Myriam Molinet

Pechkado frito

Yaako sells fried fish	Pechkado frito vende Yaako
Where was it fried? In Mazelto's frying pan	Ànde lo friyò, en la sartèn de Mazelto
Ah! Mazelto's frying pan is marvellous	Ah ay ke sartèn ke tyene Mazelto
Who warmed it up? It was Mr. Yaako	Kyèn se la hameò, el senyor Yaako
Yaako sells warm bread	Pan kalyente, vende Yaako
Where was it baked? In Mazelto's oven	Ànde lo kozyò, en el forno de Mazelto
Ah! Mazelto's oven is marvellous	Ah ay ke forno ke tyene Mazelto
Who warmed it up? It was Mr. Yaako	Kyèn se lo hameò, el senyor Yaako
Yaako sells parsley and coriander	Perechil i kulantro vende Yaako
Where was it grown? In Mazelto's cup	Ande lo hateò, en el fendjan de Mazelto
Ah! Mazelto's cup is marvellous	Ah ay ke fendjan ke tyene Mazelto
Who warmed it up? It was Mr. Yaako	Kyèn se lo hameò, el senyor Yaako

Judeo-Spanish
Traditional, musical arrangement Christophe Hoarau
and Paul Mindy Singer Awena Burgess

24 Adon hakol

אֲדוֹן הַכֹּל מְחַיֶּה כָּל נְשָׁמָה
יְצַּו חַסְדּוֹ לְבַת נָדִיב חֲכָמָה
לְבוּשָׁה מֵעֲנַן תֹּאַר יְקָרוֹ
וּמַשְׁפַּעַת עֲלֵי כָל הָאֲדָמָה

שְׁאוֹן גַּלֵּי גְבוּל יַמִּים תְּעוֹרֵר
וְעִם דּוֹדָהּ בְּצִלּוֹ נֶעֱלָמָה
בְּחֵן בַּעְלָהּ שְׁבָטֵינוּ תְּנַהֵל
וּמַעֲלָתָהּ מְהֻדֶּרֶת וְרָמָה

זְמִירוֹת מִכְּנַף אֶרֶץ שְׁמַעֲנוּם
צְבִי צַדִּיק בְּמִזְרָחָהּ וְיָמָּה
יְשָׁרִים הוֹלְכִים תָּמִיד בְּיֹשֶׁר
נְקִיִּים הֵם בְּלִי עָוֹן וְאַשְׁמָה

שְׁמוּעָתָם לְטוֹב כֻּלָּם בְּרוּרִים
וְלָהֶם נִכְסְפָה נַפְשִׁי בְּתֵימָה
צָרִי גִלְעָד שְׁלַח לָנוּ יְדִידִי
בְּצִיּוֹן נִשְׂמְחָה גֶּבֶר וְעַלְמָה
אָנָּא יְיָ הוֹשִׁיעָה נָּא.

Lord of All, who reviveth all souls
Be generous to Nadiv the Noble One
Cloaked in the cloud of her greatness
And the Earth's influence
She will summon waves
From the depths of the ocean
Her beloved's shadow will protect her
She and her husband will lead our tribes
Her Highness is honoured for her greatness
We have heard songs
From the depths of the Earth
About a just one from East to West
Honest people are always drawn to honesty
They shun all sin and all blame
Clearly they have a good reputation
Thus my soul revealed itself in Yemen
My friend, heal our wounds
Men and women, we will rejoice in Zion
That God protects us

Adon hakol mehaye kol neshama
Yetsav hasdo levat nadiv hakhama
Levousha meànan toar yekaro
Umashpàat àley khol ha adama
Shaon galei gvoul yamim teòrer
Veìm doda betsilo néélama
Behen baàla shevateynou tenahel
Oumaàlata mehouderet verama
Zmirot mikenaf erets shmaànoum
Tsvi tsadik bemizraha veyama
Yesharim holkhim tamid beyosher
Nekiyim hem bli àvon ve ashema
Shmouàtam letov koulam brourim
Velahem nikhsefa nafshi beteyma
Tsari gilàd shlakh lanou yedidi
Betsion nismekha gever ve àlma
Ana adonaï hoshià na

Hebrew
Lyrics and music **Shalom Shabazi**
Singers **Awena Burgess** and **Raphaële Lannadere**

Moroccan Arabic
Traditional, musical arrangement
Christophe Hoarau and Paul Mindy Singers Anita Soussana,
Nathalie Soussana, Paul Mindy and Juliet Hoarau

Sīdī hbīdī

25

Where are you my white house
My childhood home?

In the white house I look for my friend, my friend, where are you?
Where has the time gone when I lived in this great home?
Here is the rose with its thorns
I go toward the ghosts of my past
Yes there he is, my friend, he hasn't forgotten me
He returns filled with melancholy
His beautiful dark eyes took me from my mother
Yes there he is, my son, he hasn't forgotten me
I am sick, an imaginary invalid
There is my friend, there is my son, and my beauty
Where is it to be found

هَيْلا هَيْلالي الدَّار البيضاءْ دْيالي

هَيْلي هَيْلي حْبيبي دْيالي فينْ هُو

يا حسْرة على دوك الأيامْ فينْ قدُّور دْيالي

هاﻟْوردْة ها ﻟْوردْة هاﻟْوردْة بالشُّوكة

أنا جْنيَ وجْنُوني على الحاجة المشْروكة

سيدي حبيبي هاهو الزين دْيالي ها هو غْزالي ما يْنْساني

أنا جيني وَجيني وَجيني بلْغُمّة

هَدوكْ العْيُونْ الكْحلْ فرْقُوني على يَمّة

سيدي حبيبي هاهو أنا وليدي هاهو غْزالي مَايْنْسَني

أنا مْريضْ أناَ مْريضْ حَتّيَّ مرضْ مَايِّ

سيدي حبيبي هاهو سيدي وليدي هاهو غْزالي فين نصيبه

Haylalā haylālī dārʼl bayda dyāli

Haylī hayli hbībī dyālī feyn howa
Yā hasra ɛalā dūk-layyām fin qaddūr dyālī
Hā-l-warda hā-l-warda hā-l-warda bechchowka
Ana jennī wu jnnūni eal-l-hāja l-machrūka
Sīdī hbībī hā howa ezzīne dyālī hā howa ghzālī mā yensānī
Anā jīnī wa jīnī wa jīnī b-el-ghomma
Hādūk l-ɛuyun l-kūhel farqūnī ɛla yemma
Sīdī hbībī hā howa anā wlīdī hā howa ghzālī mā yensānī
Anā mrīd anā mrīd hettā mard mābiyya
Sīdī hbībī hā howa sīdī wlīdī hā howa ghzālī fin nsebū

Yā ommī, yā mālī

26

Mother, Oh Mother, Oh Mother
Your name is always on my lips
My treasure, my treasure, oh you, king of the home
May God touch you and lift up your soul

Yā ommī, yā ommī, yā ommī
Wa semek dāyman fi fommī
Yā mālī yā mālī yā rayes al-dār
Khallīk rabbī tɛich lī zāyd laɛmar

يا أمي يا أمي يا أمي
وأسمك دايما في فمّي
يا مَالي يا مَالي يا رَايْس الدَّار
خَليك رَبي تَعيش لي زَايْد العمْر

Algerian Arabic
Traditional, musical arrangement
Christophe Hoarau and Paul Mindy
Singer Patrick Assoune

27 Ay le lule

שלאָף מײַן קינד.
וװיל איז דעם װאָס האָט אַ מאַמע
און אַ וויגעלע דערצו
אײַ לע לולע לולע לו, אײַ לע לולע לולע לו.

אַלעס קען מען מען, קען מען קויפֿן
אַלעס קריגט מען אויף דער וועלט,
נאָר אַ מאַמע, זי איז איינע
זי איז איינע אויף דער וועלט.
אײַ לע לולע לולע לו, אײַ לע לולע לולע לו.

Ay-li, lyu-li, ay-li, lyu-li
Sleep my dear one in peace
Happy is he who has a mother
And a little cradle as well
Ay-li, lyu-li-lyu

Anything can still be found
You can still get anything for money
But a mother she is one
There's just one in all the world
Ay-li, lyu-li-lyu

Ay le lule
Shlof mayn kind
Voyl iz dem vos hot a mame
Un a vigele dertsu
Ay le lule lule lu

Ales ken men, ken men koyfn
Ales krigt men oyf der velt
Nor a mame, zi iz eyne
Zi iz eyne oyf der velt
Ay le lule lule lu

Yiddish
Lyrics David Einhorn
Musical arrangement Christophe Hoarau
and Paul Mindy Singer Nathalie Soussana

Zolst azoy lebn

28

Madam, take care and enjoy yourself
While I rock your baby

Ay lyu lyu, shush, shush, shush!
Your mother has gone out
Ay lyu lyu, sleep my child
She'll be back soon!

Enjoy yourself, and what of me then?
Your mother is working in the street

Other girls dance and have fun
And I have to sing and rock the baby!

Other girls get to eat sweets
And I have to wash diapers!

Zolst azoy lebn un zayn gezunt
Vi ikh vel dir un vign síkind

Ay-lyu-lyu, sha-sha-sha !
Dayn mameshi iz gegangen in gas arayn
Ay-lyu-lyu, shlof mayn kind
Di mameshi vet kumen gikh un geshvind!

Zolst azoy lebn, Síligt mir derinen
Dayn mameshi iz gegangen in gas fardinen

Andere meydelekh tantsn un shpringen
Un ikh muz dem kind vign un zingen!

Andere meydelekh tsukerkelekh nashn
Un ikh muz dem kinds vindelekh vashn!

Yiddish
Traditional, musical arrangement
Christophe Hoarau and Paul Mindy
Singer Norig Recher

זאָלסט אַזוי לעבן און זײַן געזונט
ווי איך וועל דיר זיצן און וויגן ס'קינד.

אײַ־ליו־ליו, שאַ־שאַ־שאַ,
דײַן מאַמעשי איז געגאַנגען אין גאַס אַרײַן.
אײַ־ליו־ליו, שלאָף מײַן קינד,
די מאַמעשי וועט קומען גיך און געשווינד.

זאָלסט אַזוי לעבן, ס'ליגט מיר דערינען,
דײַן מאַמעשי איז געגאַנגען אין גאַס פֿאַרדינען.

אַנדערע מיידעלעך טאַנצן און שפּרינגען,
און איך מוז דעם קינד וויגן און זינגען.

אַנדערע מיידעלעך צוקערקעלעך נאַשן,
און איך מוז דעם קינדס ווינדעלעך וואַשן.

About the Languages

Hebrew is the oldest Semitic language of the South. The first texts of the Bible were written some 1,000 years before the modern era! In spite of its spiritual reach, Hebrew continued to exist only as a religious language after the diaspora of the first century A.D. Once the Zionists returned to their ancestral homeland in the 19th century, they re-appropriated Hebrew and created new words from ancient forms of the language. Today, along with Arabic, Hebrew is the official language of modern Israel and is spoken by some five million people. While its pronunciation has evolved over time, Hebrew can trace its origins back to the Phoenician alphabet. The Hebrew alphabet is made up of 22 symbols. The grammar, structure and word order are similar to those of Arabic. Both languages also share a writing style that goes from right to left, in which short vowels are not indicated, except in texts used for teaching.

Yiddish derives its name from the corruption of *jüdisch*, which is German for "Jewish". Long ago, it was called *taytsh*. Today language specialists prefer the term Judeo-German, which is more precise and follows the same model as Judeo-Spanish. Created more than 1,000 years ago under the reign of Charlemagne, this dialect was originally adopted by the Jews of northern France who migrated to the Rhine Valley. A fusion language, Yiddish is derived mainly from Middle German, interspersed with 10% Hebrew words and 10% Slavic words. It is written from right to left and uses the same alphabet as Hebrew. Yiddish is used in everyday conversation by Eastern and Central European Jews, known as Ashkenazi, and co-exists with Hebrew-Aramaic, which is reserved for religious use. Prior to World War II, eleven million people spoke or understood Yiddish; no other Jewish language has achieved this degree of popularity. After the war, however, many survivors left for new countries and abandoned Yiddish in favour of the national language. Nonetheless, Yiddish remains the mother tongue of some communities in Israel, North America and Argentina and has infiltrated other languages, such as New York City slang, which is peppered with it. Modern Yiddish has several pronunciations and vocal distinctions between Northern and Southern dialects. For example, in the song *Yome, Yome*, Lithuanian Jews would say *vous dos* while Polish Jews would say *vous dous*. In this album, we have adopted a standard Northern Yiddish pronunciation.

Judeo-Spanish (originally called Djudezmo, Djidyo or Espanyoliko) originated in medieval Spain. After the expulsion of the Jews from Spain in 1492, the language spread to the major urban centres of the former Ottoman Empire, northern Morocco and Vienna. This diaspora explains the variations represented by two major groups: Judeo-Spanish of the Ottoman Empire and Haketiya of northern Morocco. Today Haketiya is spoken by a widely scattered community and is in danger of disappearing. Judeo-Spanish, on the other hand, has prospered and developed in the communities of the former Ottoman Empire by integrating Turkish, Romanian or Bulgarian and, later, French and Italian influences. As in the case of Yiddish, World War II dealt a serious blow to its continued development. Judeo-Spanish is spoken sporadically today in some major European cities (Brussels, Paris) and in the United States (Seattle, Los Angeles, New York City and Miami), and more consistently in the communities of Izmir and Istanbul in Turkey, and Tel Aviv and Jerusalem in Israel. Until the 20th century, Judeo-Spanish used the Hebrew alphabet. Beginning in the 1920s, under the influence of European culture and language reform in Turkey, Judeo-Spanish began to be written in Latin characters. In the last three decades, various graphic standards have been imposed in the different countries where the language is spoken and studied: Shalom (Turkey), Aki Yerushalayim (Israel, United States), CSIC (Spain) and Vidas Largas (France) which is the one used here. Judeo-Spanish also has regional variations in lexicon and pronunciation. We have attempted to reflect these in our songs; for example, speakers in Sarajevo would say *Il paridu*, while those in Istanbul would say *el parido*. Judeo-Spanish should not be confused with Ladino. As Professor Haïm-Vidal Sephiha has shown, Ladino is an artificial or calque language based on rabbinical tradition and used in the translation of sacred Hebrew passages.

Arabic's reach is tied in with the arts, letters and a religion, Islam. While Arabic continues to be spoken by more than 150 million people around the world, many dialects are in decline. The two nursery rhymes presented in this collection reflect Arabic dialects that differ greatly from region to region. The Jewish communities, whose members mainly practice urban trades, live primarily in major urban centres: Constantine, Oran, Algiers, Djerba, Tunis, Casablanca, Marrakech, Tangiers and Essaouira. In most cases, they use the dialect of the country and region in which they live, combined with some Hebrew words. Only the Jews of northern Morocco use Judeo-Spanish.

About the Songs

What do the rites and popular cultures of Jews from Europe, Asia and Africa have in common? Palestinian and Byzantine rites date back the furthest; Babylonian-Spanish (or Sephardic) and Franco-Germanic (Ashkenazi) rites are the most widely practiced today.

The nursery rhymes and lullabies in this collection have many variations, often beginning in oral traditions and put together from improvisation.

1   Erev shel shoshanim **Hebrew**
(Evening of Roses)

Contemporary Israeli poet and children's author Moshe Dor penned this lovely lullaby, which was already part of the traditional repertory. Like many lullabies, it belongs to the romantic genre to which the very young are so responsive! In the tradition of love stories, the song welcomes the newlyweds under the *chuppah*. This cloth canopy recalls the tents of the patriarchs (which were always open to guests) and symbolizes the home the married couple will build together, as well as the celestial home. The description of the garden is evocative of the Garden of Eden. A fragrant breeze gently blows, the only remnant of paradise lost. In fact, legend has it that when Adam and Eve were expelled from the Garden of Eden, all they were allowed to take with them were the smells!

2   Alevanta Sultanatchi **Judeo-Spanish**
(Get Up Sultanatchi)

This song, with its irregular (or mixed) nine-beat rhythm, comes from Bulgaria. While all the lyrics are not sung in this version, it is easy to guess that the story is about a child-mother whose pregnancy is discovered in the *hammam* (or bath). In the Ottoman Empire and the Balkans, it was traditional for women of all ages to go to the hammam on Fridays. In their *bogo* (a type of bag folded in four), they carried their bathing implements: *galetchas*, wooden sandals or clogs, and the *tas* or leather cup used to sprinkle the body with water. Sharing this bathing ritual allowed women to meet… and arrange future marriages!

3   A la una **Judeo-Spanish**
(At One O'Clock)

Every Jewish-Spanish family knows this *cantiga* or monophonic song, which dates back to medieval Spain. A blend of nursery rhyme and love song, it celebrates the cycle of life and lets little girls dream of their future life. In this way, it resembles the French nursery rhyme "Quand Fanny était un bébé" (when Fanny was a baby). Here, the choice of orchestration inspired by Flamenco music, with guitars and percussion instruments, recalls the time when Jews, Muslims and Christians lived in harmony in Andalusia before the Spanish Inquisition.

4   Dona, dona Yiddish

This melody, originally entitled *Dana, dana,* was composed by Sholom Secunda (1894–1974) for Esterke, a play written by Byelorussian Aaron Tseitlin. Torn between celebrating the 1000-year history of the Jewish people and the temptation to do nothing, this poem seems to vasilate between myth and reality, between laying all bare and liturgical pomp. Using a fairly transparent metaphor, *Dona, dona* compares the condition of a little tethered calf being led to slaughter to the deportation of the Jews during World War II. The choice of the image of the calf, the sacrificial victim of pagan rites, is intentional, but the purpose of the Shoah was not atonement. The success of the song undoubtedly lies in its powerful image and musical quality. Performed in Yiddish and English by Theodore Bikel, Joan Baez and many other artists, it has been translated around the world.

5   Ikh bin a kleyner dreydl Yiddish
(I Am a Little Dredyl)

This song, which originated in Poland, refers to the traditional dreydl (or spinning top), a long favoured toy in playgrounds. During the reign of Antiochus IV, who persecuted the Jews and banned the study of the Torah, Syrian officers paid regular inspection visits to religious schools. According to legend, when the soldiers would enter the schools, the children would quickly hide their religious books and get out their dreydls to fool them.

Four-sided dreydls were made during the Feast of Chanukkah at the *kheyder*, a religious school, from lead shavings that children collected throughout the year. On each side a Hebrew letter was written, representing the first initial of a German word. If the spinning dreydl landed on the side with the "n" for *nichts* (nothing), the player got nothing; if it landed on "g" for *gut* (good), the player won; if it landed on "h" for *halb* (half), the player won half; and if it landed on c for *schlecht* (bad score), the player lost! The letters form the acronym of a placename – Nes Gadol Haya Cham – where a miracle occurred, and serves as a reminder to Jews that they and their Temple overcame Greco-Syrian persecutions.

6   Der zeyger Yiddish
(The Clock)

This clock song tells of waiting time and plays on a child's delight at counting the hours. The characteristic "tick tock" of the clock is reminiscent of a mother's heartbeat, a reassuring element in a little one's world. Intimately tied to the organization of family life, the clock marks the major moments of each day, from breakfast to bedtime. It is found in nursery rhymes and songs the world over.

7 La parida Judeo-Spanish
(The New Mother)

This traditional song or *copla* celebrates the cycle of life. The soon-to-be mother is surrounded by women (including her mother, mother-in-law and female neighbours) who join in song to ward off evil spirits during her pregnancy, childbirth and the eight days preceding the newborn's circumcision. The lengthy series of verses details the nine months of pregnancy. Here is another verse:

Oh, ke mueves mezes travatech de estretchura
Oh, you have endured nine months of pain
Vos nasyò un novyo de kara de luna
A healthy child has been born to you
Mos biva la parida kon su kryatura
Long live the mother and child
Benditcho el ke mos ayegò a ver este diya
God be thanked for this blessed day
Ya es buen siman esta alegriya
Such joy is a good omen

In the song, the young father waits on the veranda, a covered balcony that extends around the house and opens out from every room. In front of the door leading to the birthing room, he recites the *She'he'chiyanu*, a Hebrew benediction traditionally spoken when one discovers something for the first time, as he waits for permission to enter.

8 Tchiko Ianiko Judeo-Spanish
(Little Ianiko)

When Judeo-Spanish women in the Ottoman Empire celebrated feasts or welcomed guests, they prepared varied and generously laden plates of food! Among these salty specialties were *borrekas*, cheese puffs, *tapanadas*, *almodrotes*, vegetable gratins, *albondigas*, and vegetable balls. Here Flory Jagoda unfurls memories of his childhood, when the women would allow the children to enter the kitchen to taste the food or lick the bottom of the cooking pot! In this song from the Balkans, the bouzouki (Greek string instrument) and the accordion can be heard.

9 La serena Judeo-Spanish
(The Mermaid)

This lovely lullaby, which speaks to us of love, is very popular among Eastern Judeo-Spanish Jews. There are several variants that were later blended together by subsequent performers. Its images, while stunning, are strongly evocative. The dove, which can be found in the *Song of Songs*, symbolizes tender love and loyalty. The image of the mermaid is a metaphor of desire that drives one crazy. The structure is reminiscent of some ballads of the Hispanic world, such as *Si la mar fuera de tinta*:

Si la mar fuera de tinta
If the sea were filled with ink
I los peces escribanos
And the fish were writers
Tu manerita y querer
Your ways and desires
No la escribiría en cien años
I would not have enough time
In a hundred years to write down on paper

10 Shuster Yiddish
(The Shoemaker)

This lighthearted nursery rhyme reveals a weighty social reality: access by Eastern European Jews to various core trades was strictly regulated and most had to live from small businesses. They were shoemakers (as in this song) or tailors and the like. For the often very poor members of this community, acquiring a pair of new shoes was an event! This theme is found in many children's songs, such as *Berele* or *Patshe kikhelekh*.

Shuster lends itself well to a game of see-saw: first the child is seated on an adult's knees; as they chant the nursery rhyme together, the child is bounced up and down, and then as the final words are sung, the child is gently tipped backwards.

11 A fidler Yiddish
(A Fiddler)

This song, taught in grade school, was sung during end-of-year or birthday celebrations. It helped children learn their scales and familiarize themselves with musical instruments, the most typical in Jewish music being the fiddle. Two examples of the popular image of the little Jewish boy and his fiddle in literature are Joseph Green's popular Yiddish musical comedy *Yidl mit'n fidl* (1936) and I. L. Peretz's (1852–1915) *Metamorphosis of a Melody*, which includes the following: "In the Kiev region, no home is without a fiddle! A well born child always has a fiddle and is expected to know how to play it. If you're wondering how many men there are in a family, just look at the walls and count the number of fiddles hanging on them!"

12 Durme, durme Judeo-Spanish
(Sleep, Sleep)

This lullaby comes from the medieval Castilian repertory; however, closely related versions exist in the Judeo-Spanish repertory. The song contains typical Judeo-Spanish motifs: the *echkola* or kindergarten, where young children learned to read and write Hebrew with the Rabbi (*hakham*), and the *plasa* or market square, where all kinds of goods were traded and sold, including fabrics, jewelry and knick-knacks. As with many other nursery rhymes, the mother feeds her son dreams of a glorious future.

13/14 Otcho kandelikas / Khanuke
(Eight Candles / Chanukkah) Judeo-Spanish

These two pieces are sung during the popular feast of Chanukkah, the Festival of Lights, which is celebrated during the third month of the Jewish year, which falls between November and December on the Gregorian calendar. Chanukkah commemorates the victory of Judah and the Maccabees over the army of Greco-Syrian emperor Antiochus IV and the miracle that occurred on that day. After liberating the desecrated Temple in Jerusalem, Judah and his companions sought to light an oil lamp to rededicate it but found only a single vial of holy oil, barely enough to light the temple for one day. Miraculously, however, the oil did not run out and the candles remained lit for eight days!

In commemoration of the miracle of the lighting of the Temple, the feast of Chanukkah lasts eight days and eight nights. Each night, starting from right to left, a candle is lit in a candlelabra, called a *menorah*. The ninth candle, which is also the smallest and is called the *shammus* or servant, is used to light the eight other candles. This ritual is accompanied by songs, games, such as the dreydl, and presents. Children occupy a place of honour. The lighting of the candle is followed by copious meals during which Ashkenazi Jews feast on *latkes*, or grated potato pancakes, while Moroccan Jews enjoy *sfenjs*, sweet donuts.

15   Bibhilou/Etmol/Lekha dodi   Hebrew
(In a Hurry/ Yesterday/ My Beloved)

Here, strung together in a single band, are three Hebrew songs linked to liturgical rites. The first is an ancient song that contains an Aramaic phrase: *Ha lahma anya. Bibhilou* (Morocco) and *Etmol* (Algeria, Tunisia) are sung during the Feast of Pesach, or Jewish Passover, which commemorates the flight from Egypt, the end of slavery and the birth of the people of Israel. The Feast of Pesach lasts eight days. On the first two nights (the first night in Israel), family and friends gather and invite guests who are alone to join them at the table for the Seder meal. Thus begins a closely ordered ritual and meal during which the *Haggadah* is read, recalling the exodus from Egypt.

Passover is centered on the children, and every effort is made to keep them awake to take part in the various rituals. During the *afikoman*, the head of the household hides half a *matzo*, or unleavened bread made of flour and water, and the children must find it to receive a present. The Seder Plate, which is raised above the head of each guest at the table, contains symbolic food. In addition to matzos, these include: *charoset*, a mixture of dates, nuts and figs that represents the sweetness of freedom rediscovered after years of slavery; a hardboiled egg which symbolizes the destruction of the Temple and the cycle of life; a roasted lamb shankbone which symbolizes the Pesach offering of lamb; and bitter herns and salt water which recall the tears shed by the Hebrew slaves. These solemn and joyous moments are firmly rooted in the collective memory.

The two verses of *Lekha dodi* correspond to the first and last verses of a poem by Rabbi Salomon entitled "*Alkabets Ha Levi*" (1505–1584). Along with other melodies, this song is sung during Sabbath on the Friday night before the Kiddush, the blessing of God's name and the wine at the start of the meal. On a white tablecloth, the lady of the house places a cup and two loaves of braided egg bread (*challah*) covered with a linen cloth for the *Motsi* or blessing of the bread. She lights two candles: the first for Israel and the second for other nations. The text recalls that the Rabbis of Safed, the holy city of Palestine, led processions Friday afternoon across the fields to welcome the Sabbath Queen, called the bride.

16 Tchitchi Bunitchi Judeo-Spanish

Finger games exist in most cultures. This one begins with the little finger, called *tchitchi* in Judeo-Spanish or "baby finger.". *Bunitchi* is a linguistic invention, created for rhyme and rhythm. The adult sings along with the child and, as the rhythm of the words progresses, grabs each of the child's fingers in the following order: first the little finger, then the ring finger (called lord of the ring), then the middle finger, then the index finger, and finally the thumb. Upon hearing the last words, "*A la bokita di mi ijika,*" the child sticks his thumb in his mouth. The lyrics of this nursery rhyme also teach little ones about the respect that must be shown to the Rabbi.

17 Nani, nani Judeo-Spanish
(Sleep, Sleep)

As with *Durme, durme, Nani, nani* comes from the medieval Castilian repertory. Neither of these lullabies has elements proper to the Judeo-Spanish culture. In *Nani, nani,* for example, the husband is a farmer; Jews, however, did not work the land. While some may have cultivated grapes at the foot of Bulgarian towns in the past, most Jews practiced urban or itinerant trades. But the theme of this lullaby, also found in Turkey and the Balkans, is universal: a mother gives in to an intimate moment with her child and begins to recount her conjugal misadventures and husband's infidelity! The cradle has always been conducive to sharing confidences.

18 Yome, Yome Yiddish

There are several variants of *Yome, Yome*. The most recent was published in 1912 by Y. L. Cahan in a major repertory of traditional children's songs. One of the earlier versions appears in the form of a dialogue between a mother and her friend Yome, in which she confides her inability to watch her daughter grow up and understand her. The girl is not satisfied with a new hat or new shoes: she wants a fiancé! As often is the case with the traditional repertory, the song has evolved into a mother-daughter dialogue, sometimes sung in counter response. Note that the trades represented in the song, shoemaker, milliner, and tailor (mentioned in the third verse but not sung on the enclosed recording) were among the most practiced and widespread among Eastern European Jews. *Yome, Yome* is reminiscent of other foreign songs: in England, *Whistle, Daughter, Whistle*; in Germany, *Spinn, spinn, liebste Tochter*; and in Poland, *Dziwna, dziwna, oj dziwna ja matke mam*.

19   Yankele Yiddish

This lullaby was written by one of the last great Yiddish poets, Mordecai Gebirtig (1877–1942). In the 1920s, his songs, *Reyzele, Motele, Moyshele* and *Es Brent Briderlekh* were sung on both sides of the Atlantic Ocean and were largely popularized by stars of Yiddish theatre such as Molly Picon. *Yankele* was part of the standard repertoire of American, Russian and Israeli performers. The song features a theme common to many Jewish lullabies: a young boy's passage from childhood to adulthood. The little boy will grow up and go to school to learn *Kumesh* (Torah) and *Guemara* (oral law laid down in the latter part of the 6th century) and will finally become an erudite merchant who will be the pride of his parents!

20   Sara la preta Judeo-Spanish
(The Black One)

This satirical song originated in Turkey, where residents of the Jewish neighbourhoods of large cities amused themselves by making up humorous little songs that poked fun at a person; for example, a school teacher or a neighbour. Children formed a circle or joined hands and danced as they sang in a joyous and lively tempo.

21   Hachafan hakatan Hebrew
(The Little Rabbit)

This simple nursery rhyme, based on a Western melody, belongs to the repertory of post-1948 Israel. It is sung in *gan* (kindergarten): children form a circle and mimic the sneezes of a little rabbit that has caught a cold. Like *Jonathan a katan* or *Numi numi*, the lullaby is used in France to teach Hebrew to young children.

22   Lyalkele Yiddish
(Little Doll)

This song, also known as *Vig lid* (lullaby), was composed by Leon Dreytzel (1895–1914), a Russian musician who immigrated to Argentina. Very popular among Eastern European Jews in Buenos Aires, it testifies to a Yiddish culture that lives on today in the four corners of the world! The topic of children is addressed in an original way: a little girl is compared by her mother to a doll. In fact, whenever the sex of a child is mentioned in Yiddish lullabies, it most often refers to little boys, the "kings of the home"!

23   Pechkado frito   **Judeo-Spanish**
(Fried Fish)

This traditional piece from northern Morocco recounts how daily life was organized in Jewish neighbourhoods. Bread was baked and Sabbath meals were slowly simmered in the baker's oven. Mutual aid and resourcefulness were necessary to feed the numerous and sometimes poor families. In popular tradition and literature, this era gave rise to such colourful characters as Albert Cohen's *Mangeclous* (Nail-eater)!

24   Adon hakol   **Hebrew**
(Lord of All)

Although 50,000 Jews emigrated from Yemen to Israel between 1948 and 1950, there is still a small scattered Jewish community in the country. It is thought to date back to the fall of Jerusalem in 70 A.D. Because of its relative isolation, this community has kept its religious and cultural traditions relatively intact. *Adon hakol* was composed by the poet Rabbi Shalom Shabazi in the 17th century. This song speaks of the hope, passed on from generation to generation, of returning to the Promised Land. It is also the subject of a Pesach prayer and the songs that accompany it. This song evokes Nadiv the Noble One, the daughter of Abraham and incarnation of the people of Israel, who will guide the Jews of Yemen to Zion, one of the hills upon which Jerusalem was built.

25   Sīdī hbīdī   **Moroccan Arabic**
(The White House)

This song, which features traditional Eastern ululations, is highly prized by Moroccan Jews. It accompanies all festivities: circumcision, Bar Mitzvah (a boy's religious passage into manhood) and marriage. In spite of its joyful tempo, it is a melancholic song, evoking a return to childhood: gatherings in the white family home and first emotions. The graphic image marvelously conveys nostalgia for the Moroccan countryside, the landscapes of the past. Beloved faces are conjured up as if in a mirage: the face of a mother, that of a friend, along with these questions: Have you forgotten me? What will I find again? The song is written in Moroccan Arabic. Moroccan Jews speak a dialect of Arabic in their daily lives, reserving Hebrew exclusively for religious practice, and often learning French in school (a legacy of the Protectorate). Their music is reflective of the three cultures: the nursery rhymes and songs they learn in school are in French; the songs sung during festivities or Sabbath are in Hebrew; and traditional and sentimental music is in Arabic-Andalusian.

26   Yā ommī, yā malī Algerian Arabic
(My Mother, My Treasure)

This Algerian lullaby is in fact, a blend of two lullabies, one from Oran (*Yā ommī*) and the other from the south of the country (*Yā Mālī*). The melody is improvised in the Constantine mode. This improvisation game was very common in northern Africa. Mothers would elaborate on yalil yalil (la la la), a few words (my eyes, my sweet, my honey, and so on) or the day's events. Words were invented around a popular melody to lull children to sleep. A mother would hold her child close to her chest and stroke its back while rocking back and forth, thereby reproducing the movement used in prayer.

27   Ay le lule Yiddish

There are several versions of this lullaby, also known as *Nor a Mame*. As in *Yiddishe Mamma* and many other songs, the mother, who remains the vital conduit of the Jewish identity, tradition and general knowledge, is the central figure. Originating in Poland, *Ay le lule* was sung by Khaytshe Lerman in Aleksander Ford's film *Mir kumen on* (1935) and performed again by her granddaughter in Australia. All Jews of Polish origin love to sing this air, which indelibly marked their childhood.

28   Zolst azoy lebn Yiddish
(Enjoy Yourself, Madam)

This old traditional song from Warsaw was published in its entirety in 1928 by Y. L. Cahan. It was retitled The *Babysitter's Song* by singer and ethnomusicologist Ruth Rubin Chanson to reflect its theme, which remains modern and relevant today! The lyrics express the feelings of a young girl whose plans are thwarted. While she would prefer to be out dancing and having fun, she is stuck babysitting the child of a woman who is out working in the streets. The initial notes of the introduction, played on the clarinet, are borrowed from the famous *Mazal Tov*, a song of good luck to young newlyweds. Here a Klezmer style is combined with the cadence of the hora, an Israeli circle dance whose steps closely resemble those of the sirtaki.

About Klezmer Music

The word *klezmer* is a contraction of two Hebrew words: *kley* (instrument) and *zemer* (song). Klezmer music is the traditional music of Eastern European Jews. Inspired as much by secular songs and popular dances as by *nigunim* (simple religious melodies) and Jewish liturgy (*hazanut*), it expresses the entire range of human emotions, from joy to despair, devotion to rebellion, contemplation to exhiliration, and, of course, love! It is said that Klezmer music has the ability to make people laugh with tears (*lakhn mit trern*) and the evocative power of religious songs. In Alicia Svigals' words: "It's so close to the cantorial (synagogal) singing that it seems religious, even if it's not."

Because of its origins, the most popular language of Klezmer music is Yiddish, but it also draws on other languages. One can detect Oriental, Gypsy and Russian accents as well as echoes of typical Eastern European music. Klezmer music is characterized by heterophony, ornamentation, special phrasing and augmented-second intervals.

The main Klezmer instruments are the clarinet, whose sound closely resembles that of the *shofar*, the ram's horn used during Rosh Hashanah (Jewish New Year) and Yom Kippur (Day of Atonement) services; the violin, "the soul of Jewish music"; the accordion, also found in Russian and Gypsy music; the double bass; and a later addition, the guitar.

Record producers **Jean-Christophe Hoarau** and **Paul Mindy**
Song selection, notes and vocal arrangement **Nathalie Soussana**
Illustrations **Beatrice Alemagna**
Recorded at **Studio Toupie**
Mixed and mastered by **Yann Coupier**
Graphic design **Stéphan Lorti** for **Haus Design**

Singers
Awena Burgess, Raphaële Lannadere, Norig Recher, Patrick Assoune,
Esther Bluwol, Muriel Hirschman, Isabelle Marx, Paul Mindy, Myriam Molinet,
Anita Soussana, Nathalie Soussana, Laura Drouillard, Juliet Hoarau,
Gabrielle Maalouli, Avran Thepault, Milena Thepault

Musicians
Paul Mindy daf, riqq, darbouka, udu, cajon, pandeiro, guimbarde
Jean-Christophe Hoarau guitars, oud, mandolin, bouzouki, bass,
percussion, vocals
Jasser Haj Youssef violin
Khadija El Afrit qanoun
Mohamed Nabil Saied oud
Christine Laforet accordion
Jason Meyer violin
Yannick Thepault clarinet

Translations
Yiddish Hilda Even Haïm, David Abihsira,
Belinda and Jonathan Naamat, Pauline Bebe, Gilles Rozier,
Sharon Bar-Kochva, Nadia Dehan, Isabelle Marx, Denise Wolnerman
Arabic Vanessa Pfister-Mésavage, Gaëlle Colin
Judeo-Spanish Aïcha Idir-Ouagouni, Anita Soussana,
Patrick Assoune, Riad Abada
French to English Services d'édition Guy Connolly

Acknowledgments
Paris Yiddish Center and **Medem Library** (medem@yiddishweb.chauxcom),
Blanche Belfer, Arielle Sion and Choulem Rosenberg,
B Gilles Fru at Buda Musique
Flory Jagoda for *Tchiko Ianiko* and *Otcho kandelikas,*
Jacintha for writing the second voices on *Lyalkele* and *Ikh bin a kleyner dreydl*
Hilda and Sarah Even Haïm, Marlène Samoun, Françoise Tenier,
La lettre sépharade (lettre.sepharade@wanadoo.fr),
Jean Carasso, Viviane Ezratty and Marie-Christine Varol, Maurice El Médioni,
Corinne Laporte, Frédérique Azoulay, Michel Borzykowski, Anita Soussana,
Chantal Atlani, Pierre and Sophie Fischer

www.thesecretmountain.com
©℗ 2009 Folle Avoine Productions
ISBN 10: 2-923163-46-X
ISBN 13: 978-2-923163-46-8
First published in French by Didier Jeunesse, Paris, 2005
Music works published by Lac Laplume Musique and Rageot Editions

Printed in Hong Kong, China by Book Art Inc (Toronto).